Virtual Learning

Martin Gitlin

Published in the United States of America by Cherry Lake Publishing
Ann Arbor, Michigan
www.cherrylakepublishing.com

Reading Adviser: Marla Conn, MS, Ed., Literacy specialist, Read-Ability, Inc.

Photo Credits: ©George Rudy/Shutterstock.com, cover, 1; ©Paulette Williams/flickr, 5; ©CREATISTA/Shutterstock.com, 6; ©LightField Studios/Shutterstock.com, 7; ©LunaseeStudios/Shutterstock.com, 8; ©Marzolino/Shutterstock.com, 10; ©Leonard Zhukovsky/Shutterstock.com, 13; ©Tyler Olson/Shutterstock.com, 14; ©Carballo/Shutterstock.com, 15; ©ZoFot/Shutterstock.com, 19; ©Faizal Ramli/Shutterstock.com, 20; ©YAKOBCHUK VIACHESLAV/Shutterstock.com, 23; ©Pavel105/Shutterstock.com, 24; ©HealthyTechSTUDIO/Shutterstock.com, 26

Graphic Element Credits: ©Ohn Mar/Shutterstock.com, back cover, multiple interior pages; ©Dmitrieva Katerina/Shutterstock.com, back cover, multiple interior pages; ©advent/Shutterstock.com, back cover, front cover, multiple interior pages; ©Visual Generation/Shutterstock.com, multiple interior pages; ©anfisa focusova/Shutterstock.com, front cover, multiple interior pages; ©Babich Alexander/Shutterstock.com, back cover, front cover, multiple interior pages

Library of Congress Cataloging-in-Publication Data

Names: Gitlin, Martin, author.
Title: Virtual Learning / by Martin Gitlin.
Description: Ann Arbor : Cherry Lake Publishing, [2019] | Series: Disruptors in tech | Audience: Grades: 4 to 6. |
    Includes bibliographical references and index.
Identifiers: LCCN 2019006016 | ISBN 9781534147591 (hardcover) | ISBN 9781534150454 (pbk.) |
    ISBN 9781534149021 (pdf) | ISBN 9781534151888 (hosted ebook)
Subjects: LCSH: Educational technology—Juvenile literature.
Classification: LCC LB1028.3 .G544 2019 | DDC 371.33—dc23
LC record available at https://lccn.loc.gov/2019006016

Printed in the United States of America
Corporate Graphics

Martin Gitlin has written more than 150 educational books. He also won more than 45 awards during his 11-year career as a newspaper journalist. Gitlin lives in Cleveland, Ohio.

Table of Contents

CHAPTER ONE

The Old World of Education

American students throughout history have had few or no choices about their schooling. They attended the school that was closest to them, whether it was in a beautiful or run-down building. And they were taught by teachers who may have been motivated and dedicated or crabby and scary.

Choices

Parents had two choices. They could send their children to a public school. Or they could **enroll** them in a private school, but only if they had enough money or were able to secure a scholarship. They had to ask themselves questions. Which school would provide the best education? Would a private school be worth the expense?

Teachers also had two choices: teach at a public school or a private school.

But now, there is a third option: **virtual** schools.

The University of Illinois is credited with having created the first online learning system for its students—9 years before the internet was invented!

Many families also choose to homeschool their children because they are concerned about the quality and environment of other schools.

Before Virtual Schools

Not much had changed before virtual schools. Kids walked to school or were driven by car or bus. They always learned in a classroom. Those from wealthier families often received a better education because they either lived in a better **school district** or were able to afford private education. Teachers taught only those sitting in front of them. There was little instruction based on individual student needs and interests. Learning sources were limited mostly to textbooks.

But times have changed. Virtual learning provides fresh opportunities. It is an exciting new world for students, parents, and teachers.

According to research, about 90 percent of American school-aged children attend public school.

There are different types of public schools, including charter and magnet schools.

The Reality of Schools Today

Many teachers seek jobs in wealthier districts. The pay tends to be better and the work easier. Because of this, poorer school districts with crumbling buildings suffer even more. These schools are often forced to hire less-experienced teachers. And because of this, the students suffer as well. They sometimes aren't offered the same learning opportunities as students living in wealthier school districts or getting a private school education.

But with the introduction of virtual schools, this reality is changing. Future students will benefit from opportunities never dreamed of by past generations.

The first public school in the United States was the all-boys Boston Latin School. It opened on April 23, 1635. Among its later students was John Hancock, the first person to sign the Declaration of Independence.

Some historians say that distance learning has been around since the 1700s. The method used at this time was called correspondence education.

A Little History

The **technology** behind online learning is relatively new. But the idea of distance learning is not. It was born more than 150 years ago in England.

Teachers there sent lessons and received completed assignments from students by mail. The only problem was time. It took a long while for students to receive assignments and for instructors to return them. But it was helpful to students who lived great distances from school. After all, any mode of transportation then was slow by modern standards.

Online education got its start well before the internet. The internet was created by the U.S. Department of Defense in 1969 and wasn't available to the public until 1991. But the University of Illinois allowed students to take courses off computers in 1960. This was done through what was called Programmed Logic for Automatic Teaching Operations (PLATO). The program operated on thousands of computer terminals around the world. It launched many social network concepts popular today, such as message boards, chat rooms, and screen sharing.

CHAPTER TWO

The Online Options

Modern education has not added just one choice for students. Or for parents. Or for teachers. The options are many for all of them.

All that is required for an online education is an internet connection. Lessons, tests, and assignments are provided in a virtual platform. Students interact with teachers face-to-face through video meeting **software**. That is also known as virtual learning.

The Changes

Online education has created huge changes. Parents do not need to drive their kids to school. Students can take courses from home instead. Smaller classrooms result in more individual instruction for kids in schools and online. Having fewer teachers means schools need smaller operating **budgets**. And that lowers the burden on **taxpayers**.

Virtual schools offer students who compete in highly competitive sports, like gymnastics, a more flexible schedule.

E-Learning

Another online option is e-learning. There is a small difference between online education and e-learning. E-learning can be achieved online from home. But students can also attend school for the e-learning experience. Teachers might be in the same building. But they interact with students only through the internet.

E-learning takes advantage of both old and modern methods. Students could still do assignments or take tests with pen and paper. But they might snap a photo of their work with their phones and send it to the teacher for grading.

Online learning is customizable to the student.

Distance Learning

Online learning has been called distance learning. But there is a difference. Online learning can be done at any level of education. Distance learning is related mostly to college students. Foreign students take courses offered by American universities online without traveling away from home.

Not all distance learning is done by foreign students. Many American students take online classes offered by schools in other parts of the country. They simply prefer not to move to their campuses.

Critics believe that online learning can cause some students to fall behind if left unsupervised.

Blended Learning

Students who want to benefit from both classroom and online education can combine the two. That is called blended learning. It requires a strict schedule. Some students visit schools only in the morning or afternoon and learn online the rest of the day. Others spend entire school days in the building but are instructed online on other days.

The Pros and Cons

All the options make life easier. But there are drawbacks to any online learning. A big one is that it reduces a student's social life. One joy of a classroom education is creating and maintaining friendships with fellow students. Another is developing a close relationship with teachers. Neither benefit is likely when learning from home.

Students and parents must understand the positives and negatives when making choices about education. The good thing is that at least they now have choices.

Evening the Playing Field

Many school districts have complained in recent years about the lack of teachers. Online education could solve that problem.

Classroom learning requires one teacher for a small number of students. The result is that schools must hire enough teachers to fill all their classrooms and courses. The shortage means that the best teachers can choose to work at private schools or at schools in wealthier areas. Schools in poorer neighborhoods often struggle to find high-quality teachers.

This is especially true with math and science teachers. Schools have complained that there are not enough of them to go around. Some schools cannot find suitable teachers for certain subjects.

Online learning has the potential to fix that issue. It gives teachers career options. Online instructors teach thousands of students at once. This gives kids from the poorest areas of the country access to the finest instructors. For instance, a school might be without a biology teacher. That school can connect to an online biology program with a teacher who is teaching thousands of students at once. While that specific teacher may not necessarily be the one to answer a student's question, many programs have other instructors or aids that will assist in answering any questions.

CHAPTER THREE

Why Online Learning Works

No two students are alike. Intelligence levels vary greatly. Some are more motivated to learn than others. One child might embrace science. Another prefers history. Another enjoys reading and writing. Another is great at math.

These are not the only differences among students. Their living situations differ. Some come from two-parent homes. Others live with just one parent or a caretaker. Some can walk easily to school. Others live miles away. Some students have special needs that make it difficult to attend a regular school. Some students may be more advanced than other students their age and may require higher learning standards.

Better Choices

Weighing today's different education options is like trying on clothes at a store. Parents and students can explore options and decide which fits best. Kids with a parent or caretaker at home might choose online learning. Those who live far from a school might do the same. E-learning within the classroom might also be an option. Or children can choose a **traditional** education.

There are even choices within the online learning option. Such programs can provide a full course load. Or students can add a course or two to what they take in a classroom. They can take classes not offered in the local school. Or they can take a summer course online to gain **credits**.

Pace Yourself

Online education allows students to learn at their own pace. A student who is highly skilled in math can take algebra or geometry at an earlier age. A person who struggles with science can take his or her time with the course. These options are often not available in traditional schools. The unfortunate result of many of these traditional schools is that some students either don't reach their full potential or fall behind.

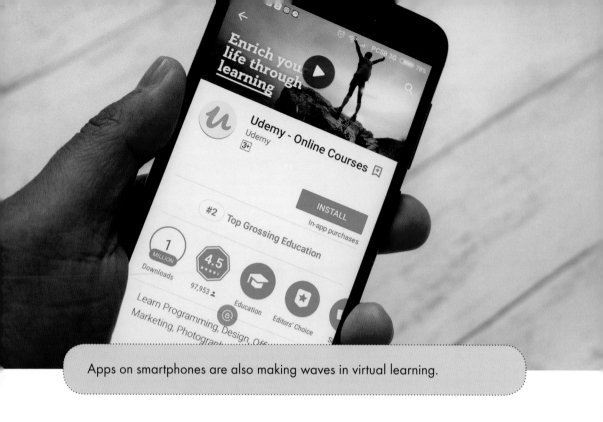

Apps on smartphones are also making waves in virtual learning.

A Whole New World for Teachers

The new world for students means a new world for teachers as well. As the number of students learning from home grows, fewer teachers are needed in traditional classrooms. But the demand will also grow for teachers to instruct online programs. They will still be needed to create lesson plans. They must interact with students through email and instant messaging. And they will always be required to grade assignments.

Online learning is in its infancy. But it has already affected millions of lives. American education will never be the same.

One advantage to online learning for teachers is that they can instruct from home. That helps those with young children. These teachers can take care of their kids and avoid paying for babysitters or preschool.

Shrinking Support Among Academics

A report issued in early 2016 revealed that American colleges were not thrilled with online education. A **survey** taken by Babson Survey Research Group showed shrinking support from **academics** despite soaring online enrollment. The number of college students taking online classes had reached nearly 6 million by that time. That number had been growing consistently for more than a decade. More than one in four college students were taking at least one online course when the survey was conducted.

The survey reported that just over one in four academic experts gave the value of online learning a high grade. In addition, the number of academic leaders who considered online education important to the future of their schools had dropped considerably over a one-year period.

The report came with a warning: The negative shift in opinion was mostly from smaller colleges. The report stated that many of them had no intention of adding online courses but that their views will have no major impact on the future of online or distance college education.

CHAPTER FOUR

An Upward Trend

Nobody is sure exactly how many students from kindergarten through high school have taken classes online. What is certain is that the number continues to grow.

A Jump in Online Learning

Two surveys indicate a rapid rise in online learning. The Evergreen Education Group estimated that nearly 3 million online courses were taken during the 2014–2015 school year. Twelve years earlier, the U.S. Department of Education estimated that just 300,000 courses were taken online. That's a big jump!

One motivation for students is credit recovery. This is when students take an online course to gain credit for classes they previously failed. By 2011, nearly all schools offered credit recovery courses to their students.

From shy students to students with specific needs, online learning offers opportunities for all students to learn.

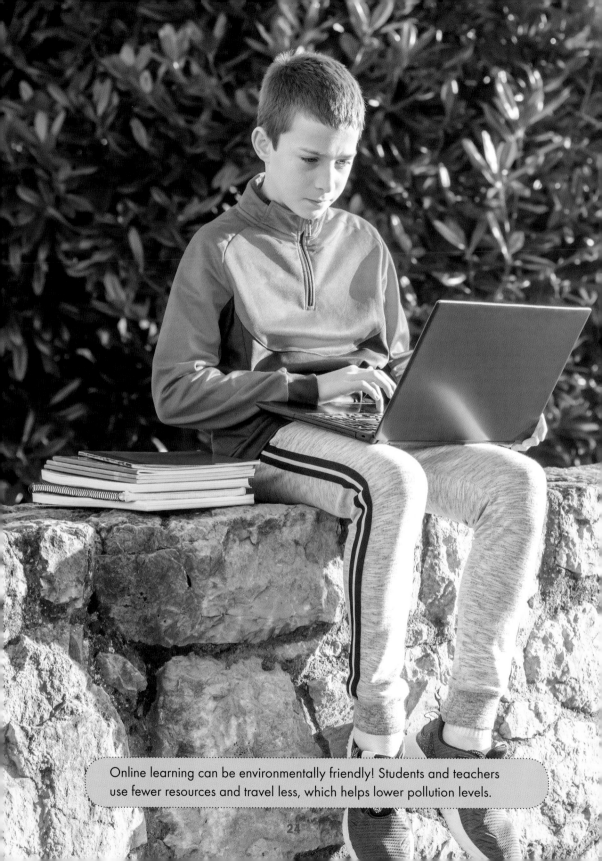

Online learning can be environmentally friendly! Students and teachers use fewer resources and travel less, which helps lower pollution levels.

Still Up in the Air

Early reports on online learning have been mixed. The National Education Policy Center claimed that students taking virtual classes performed the same or only slightly better than those in traditional classrooms. The study did indicate that taking courses online improved attendance. Students were a bit more **engaged** in their education. But the same study was unclear about how much online learning helped struggling students.

Some states require that all students take at least one online course before graduating high school. Among them are Alabama, Arkansas, Florida, Michigan, and Virginia. Other states encourage students to do so.

As of 2019, a little over 21 percent of K-12 public schools offered at least one online course.

Choosing to Learn Online

Parents have expressed a wide range of reasons for choosing online learning for their kids. The most popular are easier scheduling and discontent with the local school. Parents cited home as a safer learning environment. They also liked being able to be more involved in their children's education. Some parents even referred to bullying in school as a reason to keep their kids within eyesight.

Will physical schools become a thing of the past someday? Will all students eventually learn online? No one really knows. But what we do know is that online learning is certainly the wave of the future.

The Power
of Commitment

Some things will never change. Hard work and dedication will always be key ingredients to success. That will be true whether students listen live to a teacher in a classroom or on a computer at home.

This was confirmed in a 2014 study of Wisconsin students. The study found that students who were more engaged in their online work performed better. Those who spent more time logged into their learning system received better grades. Those who accessed more lessons and posted more often to online discussion boards did well with their academics.

The study revealed other facts about online learning. It concluded that the most effective online courses featured quality face-to-face time with instructors.

Timeline

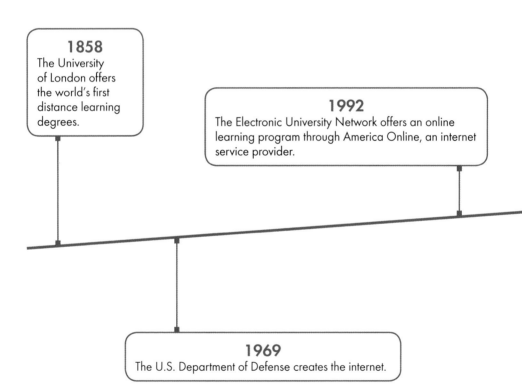

1858
The University of London offers the world's first distance learning degrees.

1992
The Electronic University Network offers an online learning program through America Online, an internet service provider.

1969
The U.S. Department of Defense creates the internet.

2014
Almost all public colleges offer online programs.

1997
California Virtual University begins to offer more than 1,000 online courses.

2009
The number of students taking at least one course online reaches 5.5 million.

2007
The first advanced interactive online learning system is launched.

Learn More

Books

Bedford, David. *Once Upon a Time … Online: Happily Ever After Is Only a Click Away.* Bath, England: Parragon, 2016.

Oakley, Barbara, and Terrence Sejnowski. *Learning How to Learn: How to Succeed in School Without Spending All Your Time Studying.* New York, NY: TarcherPerigee, 2018.

Websites

ABCya
www.abcya.com
This website features educational games for younger students.

Funbrain
www.funbrain.com
Students up to 8th grade can play games and learn on this online site.

Glossary

academics (ak-uh-DEM-ikz) people who teach at a university or college or does research

budgets (BUHJ-its) amounts of money available for a purpose

credits (KRED-itz) units of academic work gained toward a degree

engaged (en-GAYJD) being occupied in an activity

enroll (en-ROHL) to sign up to attend a school

school district (SKOOL DIS-trikt) an area or region containing the schools that a school board is in charge of

software (SAWFT-wair) programs and related information used by a computer

survey (SUR-vay) information gathered from people about their views or feelings

taxpayers (TAKS-pay-urz) people who pay or are responsible for paying a tax

technology (tek-NAH-luh-jee) use of science to solve problems

traditional (truh-DISH-uh-nuhl) custom handed down from previous generations

virtual (VUR-choo-uhl) artificial environment experienced through sights and sounds provided by a computer

Index